For Willie

Also published by Ruwanga Trading:

The Whale Who Wanted to be Small
The Wonderful Journey
A Whale's Tale
The Gift of Aloha
The Shark Who Learned a Lesson
Gecko Hide and Seek
The Brave Little Turtle
Tikki Turtle's Quest
Happy as a Dolphin, *A Child's Celebration of Hawai'i*
The Pink Parrot *(available as an e-book)*
How the Geckos Learned to Chirp
The Rainbow Mermaids of Hawaii

For more information and fun activities, visit Gill's website:
www.HawaiianChildrensBooks.com

First published 1993 by Ruwanga Trading
ISBN 978-0961510268
Printed in China by Everbest Printing Co., Ltd

BOOK ENQUIRIES AND ORDERS:
Booklines Hawaii, a division of The Islander Group
269 Pali'i Street
Mililani, Hawaii 96789
Phone: 808-676-0116, ext.206
Fax: 808-676-5156
Toll Free: 1-877-828-4852
Website: www.islandergroup.com

The Goodnight
Gecko

**written and illustrated by
Gill McBarnet**

On a faraway island . . .

Near a big green mountain, by a golden beach
there was once a little red house.
In the little red house lived a mother, a father . . .

. . . a sister, a brother . . .

and a gecko family.
There was a mother gecko, a father gecko and two little geckos. When the first little gecko hatched out of her egg, she did what all new geckos are supposed to do. She wiggled away to greet the moon and the stars.

But the other little gecko didn't want to leave the warm gecko nest.
In loud chirps, he said
        "I'm not coming out. I don't like the night.
        I'll wait until day, when it's sunny and bright."
"But that is when we sleep, Little One," said his mother.
"We sleep by day, and come out at night."

"Well, I don't like the night, " said the little gecko. "I'd much rather be awake during the day, picking flowers in the forest . . .

. . . or swimming with the fishes in the bright blue sea.
So I'm not coming out. I don't like the night.
I'll wait until day, when it's sunny and bright."

"But geckos don't pick flowers or swim," smiled his mother.
" . . . so won't you come out and greet the moon and the stars?"
"Not while there are creepy shadows and creaky noises.
I don't like the dark!" Shuddered the little gecko.

"Little One!" Chuckled his mother. "Those long, creepy
shadows and creaky noises are only the coconut trees
dancing in the moonlight. There are many wonderful sights
at night. Come with me, and you will see!"

Mother gecko chirped . . .

"Goodnight to the moon and stars,
shining way up high.

Goodnight to the fragrant flowers
framing a blue-black sky."

"Goodnight to moths that flutter by . . .
. . . and to bright dew drops on webs nearby."

"Goodnight to cats that frisk and frolic.
Goodnight to bats that flip, flap, fly."

"Goodnight to owls that softly hoot,
    and shooting stars that brightly shoot."

"Goodnight to snails leaving silver trails,
Goodnight to mice with twirling tails."

"Goodnight to frogs on mossy logs,
    to creepy bugs . . . and sleepy dogs."

"Goodnight to sleepy birds who nest,
in any place that they think best."

"Goodnight to every girl and boy,
    falling asleep with a cuddly toy.
Goodnight to sister, goodnight to brother.
Goodnight to father, and to mother.
Goodnight . . ."
But Mother Gecko stopped suddenly . . .

. . . because the little gecko had wiggled up, up and away from her! There he was, high up on the window, chirping away at the top of his voice . . .
"Look at me! I've come out, and I do like the night.
I'll be here all night, in the bright moonlight!"

And because he now loved the night, and because he sang with such delight, from that night onwards, on that faraway island, in that little red house, the little gecko became known as . . .

. . . the Goodnight Gecko.